Guard Dog Mary

Doggie Tails Series

Guard Dog Mary

Doggie Tails Series

By David M. Sargent, Jr.

Illustrated by Jeane Lirley Huff

Ozark Publishing, Inc.
P.O. Box 228
Prairie Grove, AR 72753

Cataloging-in-Publication Data

Sargent, David M., 1966–
　　Guard dog mary / by David M. Sargent, Jr. ;
illustrated by Jeane Lirley Huff.—Prairie Grove, AR :
Ozark Publishing, c2004.
　　　p.　cm. (Doggie tails series)

　　SUMMARY:　Mary the dachshund gets out of the
house and goes to guard the neighbors' house while
they are on vacation.
　　　ISBN 1-56763-849-X (hc)
　　　　　　1-56763-850-3　(pbk)

　　[1. Dachshunds—Fiction.　2. Dogs—Fiction.
3. Stories in rhyme.]　I. Huff, Jeane Lirley, 1946–, ill.
II. Title.

　　PZ8.3.S2355Gu 2004
　　[E]—dc21　　　　　　　　　　　　　00-063704

Inspired by

Mary—who, although very small,
has been my protector for years.
I never knew such a small creature
could have such a wonderful impact on my life.

Dedicated to

Mary.
I love you.

Going to town was the plan for the day.
Shopping is a good way to while the day away.
The girls needed treats, chews, and a ball.
In one single store I could find them all.

TOYS
TREATS
FOOD
BED
TREATS
BIG DOGS
Old dogs
little dogs
Puppies
treats
chews
ball
TREATS

My mission complete, I headed for home.
I couldn't wait to see the girls. I hate leaving them alone.
Driving up to the house—something just wasn't right.
But what? I didn't know. I was about to get a fright.

Vera met me at the door as she always has,
With a wag of her tail and a dance of jazz.
Then came Buffy down from her chair
To see if I had any food to share.

But Mary didn't come, so I called out her name.
I thought she was hiding and wanted to play a game.
This game is a fun one called hide-and-go-seek.
But today it wasn't fair, because I didn't get to peek.

So I searched, and I peered. Then I wondered and thought,
"Where is Miss Mary? She's in a good hiding spot."
I looked under furniture, blankets, and pillows galore.
Then it hit me. Ah Ha, the doggie door.

Under the porch and in the yard I continued to look,
But to no avail. Was she taken by a crook?
The search finally led me out onto the street.
I stopped several cars but met with defeat.

"Have you seen my doggie? She's a red dachshund.
She's missing without a trace and must be found."
No one had seen her, they were all sorry to say.
So I thanked each one and went on my way.

I went over to the school and down to the park.
Once in a while, I'd stop and listen for a bark.
But nothing was heard, not a single sound.
"Oh wait," I thought. "Could she be at the pound?"

But the pound was no luck, and I began to cry.
"Where is Little Miss Mary?" I asked with a sigh.
With no luck in finding her, my heart grew heavy.
She wasn't even found playing at the levee.

As I dragged my feet toward home, I began to pray,
"Please, wherever she is, let her be okay."
To say "Amen," I looked up to the sky.
And at that instant, a movement caught my eye.

In a neighbor's window, there sat Mary.
Not a care in the world. Nope, not nary.
Seeing she was safe, I became overjoyed.
But how did she get in? I became annoyed.

"Oh no!" The neighbors left yesterday
To go on a trip.
They'll be gone all week with their dog Skip.
So through their doggie door, my head I stuck.
And I called for Mary but had no luck.

I took her fresh water and food every day,
Because in their house is where she planned to stay.
She guarded their house while they were away,
And I must smile when I think of it today.